MW01595804

AMERICAN REFUGEES

A Near Future Novella

MARCUS LYNN DEAN

Donated by the
Bartlesville Friends of the Library

American Refugees is a work of fiction. Names, characters, places, incidents, and institutions are the products of the author's imagination or are used fictitiously. Any resemblance to institutions, places, events, or persons, living or dead, is entirely coincidental.
copyright ©Marcus Lynn Dean 2020

All rights reserved. No part of this publication may be reproduced, stored in a retrieval system, or transmitted, in any form or by any means without the prior written consent of the author:
Marcus.Dean@LastDitchPress.com

The Last Ditch Press - Cedaredge, Colorado
www.lastditchpress.com

ISBN - Ebook: 978-1-7346746-5-1
ISBN -Paperback: 978-1-7346746-4-4

The
Last Ditch Press

DEDICATED
To The Memory Of My Uncle
JAMES O. DEAN
A Life Well Lived

November 2050

NO ONE WAS SUPPOSED TO GET HURT. Why couldn't he just let us get away? Shooting someone, anyone, was the last thing I ever wanted to do, but he left me no choice. Deep down, I know that isn't true. We always have a choice. Sometimes the choices we make seem inconsequential, but choices always have consequences. What choices did we make, not just me, but everyone in the world, that led to such a fucked up state of affairs? Out of all of the possible futures available in our past, why the hell did we choose this one?

~

They must still be searching for us. I wish we could just stay here forever, and I know that we can't. I know it won't be much longer before Marv leads them here. Marv will remember this ranch where we spent so many happy days in our youth. That was when Marv, my big brother, would have done anything to protect me. So many years ago, before I was branded a blasphemer and worse. Now, I am totally unforgivable. I am not one of them; I am one of the others. How did we grow so far apart? How do people like my brother Marv get so warped that they join the pogrom? That is, after all, what this is, nothing more than another pogrom in mankind's long history of trying to eradicate or exterminate the *other.*

Christians and Jews were once the victims of pogroms of the past. Now, the Aryan Christian Nationalists are determined to rid America of everyone who isn't one of them. Except, of course, the ones needed to do the jobs that none of them want to do. Unlike the original Nazi's pogrom, it's not just Jews this time. This time it's Muslims, Buddhists, non-whites, and even some who thought they were immune because they, too, called themselves Christian. Those who dared call themselves Christians while opposing the United States becoming a Christian theocracy. Those who opposed the rule of White Christian men. And then there are the rest of us, the worst of the lot; those who are secularists. We are the worst of the other, and to top it off, I'm not only a secularist, but I'm also gay. A gay man who not only wants freedom of religion, I want freedom from religion. As far as those who have taken over America are concerned, I am the worst of the lot. Or nearly the worst. Guess I could have been born Black.

I wasn't always a secularist, though I have always been gay. I was gay when I was just a child, though I didn't know it at the time. It took a few years for me to understand myself. I didn't fully appreciate my sexuality until at least junior high school, and I couldn't admit it to anyone, not even myself, until much later. Marv and I grew up in a conservative Catholic home. My mother made sure we attended mass regularly. Sometimes Dad would join us, sometimes not. Dad may have been a Catholic in name, but I think he always tended more toward the radical religious right. I think Dad was always more in tune with the Aryan Christian Nationalists than the Catholic Church. If not for Mom, he probably would have dropped out of church long before he did.

Of course, that was before the militias and extremists that became the Aryan Christian Nationalists got religion, or religion got them. I'm not sure how the *Christian* part of the ACN came to be, but I think it started way back when Trump was President. I was just a young boy when Trump's presidency brought all the crazies out of the woodwork. I didn't understand much about it at the time, but I have learned enough history over the years to know better than to give Donald Trump all of the credit for destroying American democracy. The predecessors to the Aryan Christian Nationalists were already gaining a lot of power and momentum before Trump ever came along. He and his political accomplices just gave them the nudge they needed to come together under one banner. Like a pile of kindling, the country was ready to burn. All it needed was the spark. And Donald Trump was more than willing to supply that spark.

When I was young, I didn't know the United States was in as much trouble as it later turned out to be. I was aware of how completely divided people were about pretty much everything, but I didn't understand it at all until I got a little older. I knew the part of Colorado we lived in was overwhelmingly conservative, while the rest of the state was much more liberal. What I didn't know then, any more than I do now, was why the conservatives seemed to have such a violent hatred of the liberals. The opposite didn't seem to be true. When I was fourteen, I don't think I had any thoughts at all about how religion and secularism fit into the picture. Or how much the decades-long debate over abortion and birth control was tearing the country apart. Oh, I'd heard of abortion, and I had a good idea of what it entailed. Mainly, I knew that as far as the Catholic Church was concerned, abortion was a terrible sin. It wasn't until several years later, when I was in high school and college, that I came to understand how Trump and the other Republicans before him had used the abortion issue more than any other to divide and conquer. It was the one issue they could always count on to fire up their base of religious conservative voters. It was the main issue they used to rule the Federal Government for decades, even though they never had a majority of the American people behind them. As long as they controlled the Senate and the Supreme Court, they maintained control no matter who was President.

In the twenties, when I was in school, it was hard to learn much American history that wasn't just propaganda about how special the country was; and, by extension, how special it was to be a citizen of the greatest nation on earth. I owe much of what I learned about the true history of the United States to Mrs. French, who taught me history for the first half of my senior year in high school. More than teaching me history, she taught me how to do the research needed to form my own conclusions. Mrs. French only lasted about half-way through that year before she was removed for not teaching "proper" U.S. history. She was fired for refusing to teach the government-mandated version of history that was nothing more than propaganda. I think the final straw that ended Mrs. French's career was when she taught us that the words "*under God*" were not always part of the Pledge Of Allegiance. We were required to recite that Pledge every morning, and Mrs. French didn't think *"under God"* should have been added to it. I don't know if Mrs. French was non-religious or just didn't think religion should be part of the government. Still, teaching students that America was anything but a Christian nation went against the official government version of history. According to that version of history, America was exceptional because of its founding as a Christian nation.

Mrs. French may not have been my teacher for long, but she influenced me more than any other teacher I have ever had, including my college professors. She was the only teacher I ever had who was courageous enough to teach us what those in power didn't want us to know. The one teacher who thought real history was more important than propaganda about how the U.S.A. was superior to any other nation that had ever existed. I wonder what happened to Mrs. French. I know what happened to the United States. I wonder if things would be different if we'd had more people like Mrs. French back then.

I know the merger of radical evangelical religion and extreme white nationalism coalesced into one movement during the late twenties when I was still in school. What I have never understood is how that unholy matrimony between religion and white nationalism came about. Did evangelical Christianity co-opt white nationalism, or did white nationalism co-opt evangelical Christianity? Maybe they were always on the same trajectory, and it just took Trumpism to bring them together. And then, there's the other question; how did the Aryan Christian Nationalists so thoroughly overcome the more liberal Christian religions? I guess a study of how and why the Nazis were elected in Germany a century earlier might provide some answers to that question.

I don't really remember that much about Trump himself. I was only ten years old when he became President. What I remember most from my childhood is the Coronavirus pandemic that hit when I was fourteen years old. I remember how much I wanted to play basketball with my friends. I remember how much I wanted to go to school, and how much I hated online learning. It's interesting, looking back on it now, how much I hated online learning at the time and how much of my later education came through the internet. That was back when the internet was the best source of knowledge the world had ever seen. A golden age, before social media and then the censors, turned the net into nothing more than a propaganda machine. Anyway, it wasn't until many years later that I came to understand how Trump was able to fan the flames of the simmering race and cultural wars that were consuming America.

I remember my parents arguing about what my mom called demonstrations, and my dad called riots. It must have been when Trump was running against Joe Biden for his second term in office, back when we still had real elections. I would have been fourteen years old then. My parent's conversations always went something like this:

"I'm afraid Trump's right," my dad would say. "If we elect Biden, the Blacks are going to burn down the cities, and we're going to be overrun by Mexicans."

"How can you say that?" my mother would say. She couldn't believe my father would even say such a thing, let alone actually believe it. "Trump's the one that's fanning the flames. Biden wants to put out the fires."

Even though I was only fourteen years old at the time, and we had no Black people at all in the small Colorado town where I grew up, I knew there was something inherently wrong with how Black people had always been discriminated against in the United States. From the slave trade that brought the original Black people here to the legal institutions that ensured they remained second class citizens, White Supremacy has always been the rule, not the exception. At fourteen years old, I knew it wasn't right that the police kept killing Black people. And it seemed to just keep happening, over and over again. In some ways, slavery never really ended. In the twentieth and twenty-first centuries, prisons just took the place of plantations for many Black people. Prisons became home for many Latinos, as well. When the majority of people in prisons are Black or Latino, and the majority of the population at large is Anglo, something is rotten, and it isn't in Denmark.

It wasn't just discrimination against Black people and Latinos that overwhelmed the country, either. It was discrimination against Mexicans and Latinx of all countries. It was discrimination against Oriental people, Middle Eastern people, Indigenous people, even women, and of course, anyone who wasn't a straight heterosexual. Fear and loathing of the other, xenophobia, was stoked and taken advantage of by the radical right to divide and conquer America in the early decades of the twenty-first century.

As if the pandemic and rampant xenophobia weren't bad enough for a fourteen-year-old boy in 2020, that was also the year of the ICE raid that took away my best friend. Eddie wasn't in the U.S. illegally. He was a citizen by virtue of being born here, but Eddie's parents apparently came to America illegally before he was born. Eddie's dad had worked construction since well before Eddie was born, and his mom worked at the local nursing home. I don't think she was a nurse, but some kind of nurse's assistant. Eddie's dad was one of several illegals caught by ICE at a construction site in Grand Junction. That, of course, led them to Eddie's mom, and at ten years old, Eddie had to go "home" with his parents to a country he'd never seen before.

It wasn't until later in life that I realized Eddie was more than just my best friend at the time. We played basketball together and saw each other's naked bodies in the locker room all the time. I think Eddie may have felt the same urges that I did, but we were both suppressing our sexuality at the time. Now, looking back, I'm reasonably sure that Eddie and I would have become lovers had he not been taken from me at such an early age.

It's only now that I realize how lucky Eddie was to have been deported when he was. Before he was either killed or forced to live life as a virtual slave in the United States. Mexico may have become part of the Catholic States of America since then, but I don't see how that could be as bad as the zealots that now control this country. The CSA may be a theocracy that discriminates against anyone who isn't a heterosexual male, but they're at least inclusive when it comes to race and skin color.

My brother Marv is three years older than me. He would have been seventeen that summer of 2020. We watched our parents argue more and more that summer. The stress of the election compounded by the stress of a pandemic, exacerbated by irreconcilable political differences, literally tore our parents apart that summer. We watched our parents fall apart, and we started falling apart, too. Not that Marv and I talked about it at the time. We were way too busy playing video games and basketball to talk or even think about politics. I'm sure the Coronavirus pandemic was worse for Marv than it was for me. It really fucked up his senior year in high school. Maybe Marv thought about politics more than I did, I don't know. Looking back now, I know that he always agreed with Dad while I found myself agreeing more and more with Mom. I know now, that is the summer when Marv and I both started down the paths that led to where we are today. Down the path that led to me being one of the hunted, and to Marv being one of the hunters.

Don't get me wrong, I didn't always agree with my mother. As a matter of fact, I'm sure that summer in 2020 is when I realized that I not only didn't believe in the Catholic church, I didn't believe in God, either. A psychologist would probably say I stopped believing in God when my mother died later on that fall. But I'm sure her dying from Covid just brought into clear focus what I already thought about God and religion. I could never understand how God, if he or she existed, could allow, let alone condone, so much suffering and inequality in the world. And the church's doctrine of wanting people to have more and more babies was really baffling to a fourteen-year-old boy. At fourteen, I could already see there were far too many people on planet earth.

Like most of my generation, even at fourteen years old, I felt that man-made climate change was an existential threat. I remember having two heroes when I was a pre-teen, LeBron James and Greta Thunberg. I still idolized both by that summer of 2020. I idolized LeBron, not just for his basketball prowess, but for his stance on social issues. And Greta Thunberg was doing more to bring attention to climate change than just about anyone else alive. I think that's also when I first started really thinking about over-population. When I first started thinking that overpopulation, not the industrial revolution, was the root cause of climate change.

I may have disagreed with my mother about religion, but, as time went on, I disagreed with my father about virtually everything. Dad also got sick that autumn of 2020, but he didn't die. He didn't even have to go to the hospital. He got sick and got over it. He refused to wear a mask or to change his behavior at all. There's no telling how many people my dad infected. I know Marv and I probably had the virus too, but it didn't affect us at all. Coronavirus didn't have any harmful effects on Marv and me, but the other sickness that infected my dad and Marv and much of the world that year tore us apart. I guess the best name for that other sickness is simply *Hate*. Hate and Coronavirus both spread across the globe in 2020. The vaccine that we finally got the next year stopped the Coronavirus, but there is no vaccine against hate.

~

"We have to go," I tell Dustin. "We've been hiding out here too long already."

"I know," he replies, gazing out at the pastoral view from the veranda of my grandparent's old ranch house. "It's so nice here. I wish we could just stay forever. Just you and me in our own little paradise."

Swallowing the last of this morning's energy bar, I can't help but laugh.

"Sorry, I always figured paradise would have better food than this," I say.

"Could be worse," he says. "At least we haven't starved to death."

"Not yet, anyway. But paradise is running out of energy bars and canned goods."

This little paradise is the Montana ranch my grandparents owned when I was a boy. It's the ranch where my mother grew up. My brother, Marv, and I used to spend time here every summer, and sometimes for the holidays in winter. I never did like it as much in the winter. When I was a boy, it was always cold and snowy for Thanksgiving and Christmas. Though not as cold or snowy, my mother assured us, as it was when she was a girl. Climate change had already taken a toll by then when I was young, but it has really accelerated in my lifetime. It's November already, and Dustin and I are sitting out here on the veranda in light jackets, looking out at a drought-stricken landscape. I don't remember there ever being a snowless Thanksgiving on this old ranch, but a lot has changed since I was a boy.

My grandparents' place was not a very big ranch, not by Montana standards, but it seemed vast and boundless when I was a boy. The illusion of infinite space was helped by the fact that the southern border of the property adjoined the national forest. There were several gates in the fences that separated my grandparent's ranch from the national forest land. Marv and I had access to nearly unlimited exploration whenever we visited the ranch. Grandpa taught us to ride when we were young, and we spent most of our summers on horseback exploring the national forest. My grandparent's cattle spent the summer grazing in that forest, and Grandpa would take us with him when he rode out to check the cows. Grandma would even ride along with us some of the time. Most of the time, though, it was just Marv and me riding through endless lands in a timeless youth.

I think it was '28 or '29 when my grandparents finally lost the ranch; or, more precisely, had their ranch stolen from them. Neither of them lived long after that. They had survived losing their daughter to Covid and having their Catholic faith slowly co-opted in America by the fundamental extremists. By those who couldn't abide a religion that was entirely too multi-ethnic and multi-cultural. By the time my grandparents both died, just a week apart, in 2030, the fundamentalists despised old-time Catholicism almost as much as they hated Islam. I really think it was the loss of the old family ranch that killed my grandparents, though. When the government stole the land and turned it over to Agrigov, my grandparents just couldn't stand to go on living.

Agrigov didn't just get the ranch; they also "bought" the federal government's national forest land. Acquiring as much land as possible, both federal and private, was, of course, the reason Agrigov, Inc. was formed in the first place. Originally, Agrigov was supposed to be a public/private partnership formed to manage the public lands that the federal government said it could no longer afford to maintain. That was the public face of Agrigov. What the public was told about Agrigov was very different from the deeper truth. In reality, Agrigov was just one more step toward the total corporatization of the entire U.S. government. Of all the bad things that have happened in my forty-four years of life in America, the complete takeover of the government by corporations owned by a handful of people is probably the worst. It is no longer government of the people, by the people, for the people, as once envisioned. It isn't even government for the corporations. The United States is now entirely owned by corporations. The land itself no longer belongs to we the people. Most of the United States of America is now owned by Agrigov.

"I'm surprised we haven't seen anyone from Agrigov yet," I tell Dustin. "Guess maybe they won't be around until next year when it's time to go kill an elk. I think that's all they use this place for now. Nothing more than a hunting cabin for the board of directors and their cronies."

"At least they hunt elk instead of us. And they were nice enough to leave us some food to eat," Dustin says facetiously, as he uses his spork to dig the last of the cold green beans from the bottom of the can.

"Yeah, yeah, and what wonderful cuisine it is," I say. Dustin and I have been living on cold canned goods, energy bars, and jerky since we got here. At least we didn't find the pantry empty. I just hope whoever does eventually show up from Agrigov doesn't know how much food should be here. We've been extremely careful to always burn the trash in the old burn barrel at night to avoid anyone seeing smoke from a distance. I'm reasonably sure no one will notice the barrel has a little bit more burned trash in it now than it did before, but someone might notice the missing food. If it's just Agrigov hunters, of course, they won't have any idea how much food was here. Just like they apparently had no idea there was a spare key to the back door hidden under a rock by the fence. They didn't even have sense enough to change the locks when they acquired the old house. Dustin and I didn't even need to break in.

"Agrigov may not be hunting us," I tell Dustin, "but you know as well as I do that everyone in Agrigov is also an Aryan Christian Nationalist. It's not them I'm worried about, though. Sooner or later, my brother will think to look for us here. Once he figures out that we aren't still hiding in Colorado, he'll come here next."

"Do you really think your own brother will come after you?" Dustin asks. Even after being found guilty of homosexuality and blasphemy and sentenced to death, Dustin's inherent kindness blinds him to the evil in others. Even though Marv testified against him at the trial, he just can't believe that my own brother would turn against me.

"I know he will," I tell Dustin. "If I hadn't helped you

escape when I did, Marv would have had me right in there with you. There's probably nothing he'd like more than seeing me sentenced to death."

"It just doesn't seem possible, that's all. I mean, your own brother, your own flesh and blood."

"He may be my brother, but he has never forgiven me for being gay. Let alone being an atheist. Marv was a homophobe long before he ever joined the ACN. As a matter of fact, that's probably what attracted him to the Aryans in the first place. I don't think Marv has any fundamental belief in any fundamentalist religion. Marv's just a homophobe, pure and simple. That and a racist. He'd bought into everything the radical right was selling before he even got out of high school. Marv just wants to rid the world of everyone that isn't like him. It's the Aryan part of Aryan Christian Nationalists that drew in Marv, not the Christian part."

"Why didn't he just have you arrested for having sex with a man?" Dustin asks. "That would get you the death penalty, just as much as blasphemy would."

"I've been wondering about that myself," I answer. "Maybe I was discreet enough that Marv wasn't sure he could prove it. I mean, unlike you, I didn't literally shout it from the rooftops." The memory of Dustin standing on the roof of the old courthouse yelling at the crowds below still makes me laugh. "What were you thinking?" I ask.

Dustin laughs, too. He puts his arm around me and gives me a kiss. "Guess I just thought I could change some of their minds," he says. That's what I love about Dustin. He has never stopped believing there is enough good left in people to overcome the hatred and xenophobia that has slowly destroyed our ancestors' America.

Something catches the corner of my eye. I turn to see a dust cloud rising in the distance. From this vantage point on the veranda, miles of the old gravel road that leads to the ranch can be seen snaking its way through the sagebrush-covered rolling hills. The source of the dust is hidden by one of those hills about five miles away.

"We have to go right now," I tell Dustin, getting up from the porch swing and pulling him up after me. "Hurry! Out the back, just like we planned."

I still have a slight limp, but the month spent here recuperating has done wonders for my leg. I can actually run again now, though not like I could in my basketball days. I thought I'd never be able to run again after that bullet tore through my calf muscle. It's a good thing we were already on the motorcycle and almost out of town when the bullet hit. It's even better that only one of us was shot and that it was only in the leg. We've been extremely lucky, Dustin and I; how much longer will our luck hold out? That worries me more than anything. The way I see it, each of us is only allowed a certain amount of good luck. Like a cat with nine lives, we each have a limited number of lucky breaks in this life. Just hope Dustin and I can get to Canada before our quota of good luck runs out.

Dustin and I grab our packs. "Check the bedrooms," I yell at Dustin as I quickly but carefully look over the living room and kitchen. I don't have to tell him what to check for, and this final walk-through probably wasn't even necessary. We've been meticulously planning this retreat for a whole month now. We have carefully kept the house exactly as we found it, knowing we might need to leave in a hurry and knowing we can't leave a trace of our ever having been here. We have slept in our sleeping bags on the carpeted living room floor. We haven't used the kitchen or the bathroom at all. The dust covering the kitchen counters and the table looks exactly like it did when we first stepped foot inside.

We have to get to Canada is the thought that drives me to run harder up the trail that I don't remember being this steep. I can hear Dustin panting behind me, struggling to keep up. Even running through the pain and limping, I am in much better shape than Dustin. Physical fitness has never been his greatest asset.

This is probably far enough. This trail that we've been following up the mountain is taking us due south, just the opposite direction of where we need to go. I stop running and wait for Dustin to catch up. "This way," I tell him and head west through an opening in the undergrowth. Poor Dustin. I know he wants to stop and rest, but we can't stop until we are hidden somewhere well off of the trail. My plan is to work our way through the forest to circle back to the north somewhere a couple of miles west of the ranch house. The road comes into the ranch from the east, so the farther west of the house we are, the farther we'll be away from the road and whoever it was raising that cloud of dust.

We'll have to wait until after dark to venture out of the forest into the open sage and grasslands. That will be the most dangerous part of our trek, those wide-open spaces we have to cross to get to the Canadian border. It can't be more than a hundred miles. I figure if we travel at night and spend the daylight hours hiding in a ditch or a hollow, avoiding roads and people, we should be able to get there in four or five days.

~

It was early October when I helped Dustin escape from the law in Colorado. The vibrant gold of the aspen leaves still on the trees in early November is a testament to how much the climate has changed in just my lifetime. I was last in these woods more than twenty years ago, back when most of the aspen leaves would be dead on the ground by now, not still shimmering gold on the trees. This part of the forest must have completely burned back then, probably shortly after I was last here. The new growth of mostly just aspen trees is so thick it is hard to get through. This part of the forest seems to be nothing but thousands of aspen saplings that aren't much taller than I am, with trunks just a few inches in diameter.

"Stop," Dustin gasps behind me, his voice no more than a loud, hoarse whisper. "I need to rest."

We are deep into the aspen thicket that seems to go on forever. We've come to a small opening with a tiny brook still flowing through it and a nearly impenetrable thicket of scrub oak on the opposite side of the little clearing—a nice place to sit and rest for a bit. By the time I decide it will be okay to have a short rest, Dustin has already pulled off his pack and jacket, and he is sitting beside the little stream.

"We're probably safe for a short rest," I tell him as I unsling the old Mossberg MMR rifle that I've been carrying and remove my own pack and jacket. It's hot enough that I'm sweating under the khaki jacket. Shouldn't have even had it on. Guess leaving it on before fleeing the house was quicker than trying to tie it on my pack, which is what I do now.

"Where's your gun?" I ask Dustin, seeing that he isn't wearing the pistol that I gave him. I have a pang of fear. Did he leave the gun in the house?

"In my pack," he says. "I hate wearing that thing. You know how much I hate guns."

"I know you hate guns, Dustin, but if they catch us, we need to be able to defend ourselves. What are you going to do, ask them nicely to give you just a minute so you can get the gun out of your pack?"

"What difference does it make? I could never shoot anybody, anyway."

It's a discussion we have already had far too many times. I didn't think I could shoot anyone either. I have killed a few deer, and even an elk, back when I was a teenager, but to shoot another human being seemed unfathomable. It was incomprehensible right up until I had to shoot that deputy to free Dustin.

"Look, Dustin, I didn't think I could shoot anyone, either." This isn't the first time I've told him that. It doesn't sway his opinion any more now than it has in the past.

"I still can't believe you actually killed that guy," Dustin says. Which is pretty much what he has said every time we talk about it.

"We don't know I killed him, only that I shot him." It's my standard reply—no doubt a defense mechanism to make me feel better about shooting another human being. I shot the man in the head for Christ's sake. Surely it killed him. Maybe not. People have survived head wounds before. Perhaps I'm not a murderer. Maybe I am. How many people have taken up arms and killed when they didn't think they would ever be able to do so? I don't so much regret shooting the deputy that was transporting Dustin to death row as much as I regret having no other option.

Dustin doesn't say anything, but I'm relieved to see him rummaging around in his pack to pull out the gun belt. He stands up, straps it around his waist, and smiles down at me.

"What do you think?" he asks. "Pretty macho, huh?"

I have to laugh. If there is one thing Dustin is not, it's macho. I smile back up at this man who is the love of my life. It reminds me of the first time we met.

I was a freshman at Regis in Denver. I didn't really choose to go to college at Regis; it was more like Regis chose me. At the time, with dreams of being a big-time college basketball star, I would have preferred CU or CSU, but neither school offered me a scholarship. I didn't much like living in Denver, and I didn't like college classes any more than I had liked high school. I did enjoy playing basketball, though. Long before Dustin, basketball was my first love. Before Dustin, basketball was my life. I don't think I could have survived growing up in small-town Colorado without basketball.

My Catholic heritage probably helped me get into Regis as much as my basketball ability, even though the school was working hard to separate itself from Catholicism. By the late twenties, any organization that wasn't tied to some kind of radical fundamentalism had to distance themselves from religion to survive. Looking back now, it's a wonder Regis survived as long as it did. Regis even outlasted Notre Dame and some of the other more famous Catholic schools. Once the fundamentalists decided to dismantle everything Catholic, it didn't take long for the Catholic colleges to be forced to shut down. I guess the only Catholic schools left now are up in Canada or overseas, or down in Mexico or one of the other Catholic States Of America.

Dustin wasn't a student at Regis. We met at a restaurant where he was a waiter. I was there with some girl I met at school. Funny, I can still picture her, but I can't even remember her name. Like the girls I dated in high school, she didn't mean anything that much to me other than making it easier to stay in the closet. The backlash against the gay pride movement was even stronger in the late twenties than the backlash against

Black Lives Matter had been earlier. By that fall in 2028, anything that even smelled of the Rainbow Coalition of an earlier time was open to attack. So, just as I'd done in high school, I dated girls even though I was sexually attracted to men. I guess I really did care about some of the girls I dated back then. I felt closer to some of those girls than to many of my male friends. Sometimes a date would even lead to sex. I had several sexual relationships with girls before I met Dustin. I probably would have ended up in bed with the girl I was with that night if it hadn't been for him.

I couldn't help but notice how he kept looking at me all through dinner, and I couldn't help but stare back. To say I had an instant attraction to Dustin would be an understatement. The feeling was apparently mutual. When he brought me the receipt, it was signed *Dustin,* with a phone number beneath his name. I remember I could hardly wait to get rid of the girl I was with so I could call that number. Making love with Dustin that night was my first time with another man. It made me feel whole and fulfilled for the first time ever. I'd fantasized about having sex with another man for years, but Dustin was so much more than the fantasy. For me, he was the first and the only man I've ever truly loved.

It didn't take long for word to get out that I was gay, even though Dustin and I tried to be as discreet as possible. That led to my nearly immediate dismissal from the Regis basketball team. The loss of my basketball scholarship led to my dismissal from Regis shortly after that. I moved directly from the athletic dorm at Regis into Dustin's apartment in the heart of downtown Denver, which is where we should have stayed. Why the hell I ever convinced Dustin to move back to my hometown, I'll never know. That was, no doubt, the biggest mistake I've ever made. If we had just stayed in Denver and kept to ourselves, we probably wouldn't be on the run now. Or maybe we would. That was twenty-two years ago; there is probably no place in America that's safe for gays anymore.

"What's that buzzing noise?" Dustin asks, bringing me back to the present.

It sounds like some kind of giant insect, and it takes a moment for me to realize what it is. It's the sound of a drone off in the distance.

"Quick, under here." I force my way under a thicket of scrub oak growing by the side of the little stream, scraping my arms and tearing at my clothes as I go. It doesn't matter. I have to open enough of a hole to get us both under cover.

"Ouch!" I hear Dustin complain about the brush, but at least he's right behind me.

The high-pitched whine is getting louder as I lay on my back and look up to make sure the sky isn't visible through the dry brown thicket of oak leaves and branches overhead. Satisfied that we can't be seen from above, I look down at Dustin, whose head is between my feet, looking at me as though he would like to just keep crawling up between my legs. Any other time would be great, but right now, I'm only thinking about two things. How are we going to get to Canada? And who is it that's hunting us—with drones no less?

"So, I guess it wasn't Agrigov," Dustin says as the sound of the drone fades off into the distance.

"Not unless they're hunting elk from the air. It wouldn't surprise me, but I'm fairly sure that drone is hunting us, not elk."

"Do you think they somehow knew we were at the ranch?" Dustin asks, more than a hint of fear in his voice.

It's a question I've been wondering about myself. I'm sure no one but Marv would have thought to look for us here. No one else would have had any way to connect me to this remote part of Montana. If it is Marv, he must have talked the police or an ACN militia group into searching here. But just because they're searching doesn't mean they know we have been at the old ranch house. Maybe, since they didn't find us at the ranch, they're just doing some flyovers to ensure we're not in the area.

On the other hand, if it's real police, not the ACN—what am I thinking? There's no difference between the police and the ACN. It'll be vigilantes hunting us, no matter if they're wearing police uniforms or not.

"I don't think they know we're in the area," I try to sound more sure than I am. "Probably searching just in case. Either way, I think we better not head out into the open until well after dark." The sound of the drone has completely faded away. I don't think they'll cover the same area twice. "Let's go," I tell Dustin. "We can get to the edge of the forest to wait out the rest of the day. We'll head out across the open tonight after dark."

"Ouch! God damn it!" is Dustin's only reply as he pushes himself back out of the brush.

~

I can't believe how lucky we are. There is hardly any moon, just the tiniest sliver in a black sky full of stars. The Milky Way is splashed so bright white across the sky that there's no question of how it got its name. The night air is warm. Much too warm for Montana in November. Nothing at all like the Montana of my youth.

I remember spending Thanksgiving with my grandparents one year when I was still in high school. It must have been when I was a junior. It was the first time I was old enough to drive from Colorado to Montana by myself. I don't think Dad visited my grandparents at all after Mom died. Marv, who was going to college in Alabama for some reason, didn't come home for Thanksgiving at all that year. He was probably too busy being indoctrinated into the KKK or something. Not that he would have gone with me to Montana anyway. By then, Marv and I were hardly even on speaking terms.

Anyway, there was about a foot of snow covering this whole area that Thanksgiving weekend, and I remember it being extremely cold. Not just freezing but probably well below zero. Thank God for climate change. Don't know if we could make it all the way to Canada if we were trudging through a foot of snow and sub-zero temperatures.

"Beautiful, isn't it." Dustin is looking up at that dazzling cloudless night sky, just as I am.

"It really is," I agree. I scan the beauty of the infinite stars and the milky way before concentrating on finding the big dipper and the north star, the compass that will lead us to Canada. For Dustin and me, Canada is the promised land. It is the only hope we have left in a world with fewer and fewer places for people like us.

As far as I know, Canada, Great Britain, and France may be the only three secular nations left on earth. Maybe some of Scandinavia or Australia and New Zealand might be, but I'm not sure. You can't count the Russian Federation or the Chinese Empire as secularist nations. They may not be governed by laws based on any of the old religions like most countries are, but then again, the so-called communism they practice is basically a religion unto itself. Whatever you want to call it, it is most assuredly not the communism or socialism envisioned by the likes of Marx and Lenin. No, modern communism is just another totalitarian religion, but no more totalitarian than the ACN in America or the Islamic States in the Middle East. Since the worship of Market Capitalism failed, most of the world is divided into opposing theocracies. Some of them, like the Islamic States Of The World and the Catholic States Of America, proudly exclaim their religious affiliation. Others, like the U.S.A., still cling to names that disguise their true nature.

"What if they won't let us in?" Dustin asks. Seems like he isn't happy unless he has something to worry about, even on a night as beautiful as this one.

I know what he means, though. Canada officially closed its border with the United States back in '28 when the Supreme Court brought free and fair elections and dreams of democracy to a final end. At the time, the groups that came to be the Aryan Christian Nationalists were probably the only thing that prevented America from becoming part of the Russian Federation or the Chinese Empire. In hindsight, being part of the Russian Federation or Chinese Empire might have been a better option. Who knows which is worse anymore, the Russian Federation, the Chinese Empire, or the Aryan Christian Nation of America? That is, after all, what this country should be called. The United States Of America died a slow death when I was a young man.

"Guess we'll just cross that bridge when we come to it," I tell him before correcting myself. "I should say, we'll cross that *border* when we come to it."

Dustin laughs at my feeble attempt at a joke.

"Seriously," I say, "I just hope we can sneak across the border before anyone knows we're there. And I sure hope what we've heard is true." Dustin and I have heard that the Canadians have adopted the policy that America used to use for Cubans. If they catch you before you get across the border, they have to send you back, but if you get into the country before they catch you, they'll grant you refugee status and let you stay.

"You think they'll let you stay, even if you're wanted for

murdering a policeman?" He asks.

"Wish I knew," I tell him. "Wish I knew. Let's just not worry about that until we get there." I've been worrying about that ever since I shot that deputy, but I don't want Dustin to worry too.

"Yeah, yeah, I know—we'll cross that border when we come to it. I heard that before, somewhere."

~

I don't know about Dustin, but I am totally exhausted. We have been walking all night and hiding in the daylight for two days now. Light is beginning to show up in the eastern sky. It's time to find another place to spend the day out of sight. We crossed a deserted highway a few miles back, and we've been in farm country ever since, traipsing across field after fallow field. They seem to grow a large variety of crops up here in northern Montana, mainly grains. From what I can tell in the dark, mostly wheat and corn. With the harvests all in, the fields are all just barren and empty now. There is what looks like a yard light maybe a mile to the west. That's the second one we've seen off in the distance. Probably old farmhouses that may or may not be occupied. If they are occupied, it won't be by landowners. I'm sure Agrigov owns all of this area, along with most of the state of Montana by now. Of course, they do need to have people working the land. That's probably the only people living in this part of the country anymore, farmers and ranchers working for Agrigov. Working for not much more than a roof over their head and some food on the table, like sharecroppers after the civil war. The only people doing well anymore are those at the very top; those at the top of government, the top of Agrigov, and the top of the ACN. Guess that's really not a very accurate way of thinking about it, though. After all, it's the same people at the top of all three. Actually, the three are one, sort of an unholy trinity to replace the holy Christian trinity of old.

We've come to an old, barbed wire fence surrounding a pasture, as opposed to a field. I don't see any animals in the pasture in the morning's growing light, but there is a dilapidated loafing shed at one corner of the fence.

"Looks like our hotel for the day," I tell Dustin as I crawl between the strands of old barbed wire and hold them apart for him to follow. The shed looks a lot more inviting than the ditches we've been trying to sleep in for the last couple of days.

"A regular Ritz, I'm sure," he answers.

In some ways, the old loafing shed is much better than the Ritz. For one thing, you don't need reservations, and you don't need to tip the bellhop. It has been a long time since this shelter was occupied. The horse manure covering the ground inside is as dried up as if it was old grass straw. Unlike a lot of loafing sheds, this one has walls covering most of all four sides. The south-facing front of the shed is only half-open, with a wall covering the other half. It's a perfect place to hide out for the day. Our unbelievable good luck is still holding.

"You do know that's horseshit, don't you?" Dustin asks as I roll my sleeping bag out in the corner where the old dried up manure is especially deep.

"Yep, nice and soft," I answer as I stretch out on top of my bag.

"Maybe we shouldn't both sleep at the same time, anyway," Dustin says, placing his rolled up sleeping bag against the back wall. He sits down on the rolled up bag and leans back against the rough slab wood. "I'll keep watch while you sleep, then maybe I'll be able to get some sleep while you watch."

"Umm," is about all the answer I can get out before sleep hits me.

It seems like a dream at first, or a nightmare. The sound of a swarm of giant insects or a plague of locusts somewhere out beyond my bed. My bed? Where am I? Then it comes back to me. I sit up, instantly alert. Dustin is slumped against the back wall of the shed, snoring, half on and half off of the sleeping bag that he sat down on. It must be late evening. It is nearly dark inside our shelter, but some light is still visible through the front opening and through the cracks between the slabs that make up the walls.

"Wake up." I gently shake Dustin's shoulder, wishing I didn't have to. Wishing I could just let him go on sleeping. Wishing we weren't fugitives trying to escape the only home we've ever known.

The sound of the drones, at least two of them, is diminishing, fading into the distance. They must have been fairly close when they woke me up. Were they hunting me and Dustin, or something else? They must be hunting us with drones. But how do they know where to look? Did we leave something at the ranch to tip them off?

Then I have another thought; maybe they are simply regular patrols searching for anyone who might be trying to escape to Canada. Dustin and I can't be the only ones. How many of us are there? Americans who no longer belong in America. Marginalized to the point of homelessness, seeking a better life in a new home, American refugees with nowhere left to go but north to Canada. Of course, it doesn't really matter if they're searching for us or just patrolling the border area. If they find us, the result will be the same either way.

"Sorry," Dustin says. "Guess I fell asleep."

"It's okay. We both needed to rest. Did you hear the drones?" I listen, but the sound has completely faded away.

"Drones? You mean like more than one?"

"Yeah, I think there were two or three of them, but they're gone now." I rummage around in my pack for some of the energy bars we've been living on for weeks now. "It's almost dark," I tell Dustin as I hand him one of the bars. "We better get moving again."

"But how do they know where to look for us? And how many of them are there?" Dustin seems to be talking to himself as much as to me.

"Maybe they aren't looking for us. Maybe they're just looking for anyone heading north."

The idea that they, whoever they might be, may not be looking for us specifically, seems to buoy Dustin's spirits, but

I have given myself a new worry now. What if they have silent military drones watching from thirty-thousand feet or some shit? What if they even have good enough infrared cameras to see us in the dark? I figure it must still be at least forty or fifty miles to the border. If the U.S. military is focused on preventing people from escaping to Canada, it might as well be a million miles.

"Come on, we need to cover more ground tonight," I tell Dustin, trying to put thoughts of futility out of my mind.

~

The terrain started getting worse last night. We're now getting deeper and deeper into some really rough badlands. Not what I expected, and definitely not what we needed. The meandering washed-out gullies and steep-sided ravines between mostly barren hills make it next to impossible to hike straight north. After another night of hiking, I had hoped to get to the border by morning. We must be getting close. This is the fourth night since we left my grandparent's old ranch. We haven't seen or heard anybody or anything that might be looking for us since hearing the drones a couple of days ago. There is no light yet in the eastern sky, but dawn isn't far off. Maybe there's more light than I realize. The morning sky is completely hidden by clouds. It isn't just the terrain that took a turn for the worse; the weather has deteriorated as well. The clouds started rolling in just as the sun was setting last night. Now, the sky is completely overcast.

"Are we even headed north?" Dustin asks. We've been

hiking up the sandy, gravelly bottom of a large wash, with so many twists and turns that I have no idea which way we're facing at the moment.

"Don't know," I tell him, "but we can't get out of this wash right here." We're in one of those stretches where the wash is actually a ravine, with near-vertical cut dirt banks on either side. The ravine is nearly twenty feet deep at this particular spot. "Guess we need to just keep going until we find a place where we can climb out."

I know Dustin is as exhausted as I am, but I have to pick up the pace to stay warm. Not only has it been getting colder, but it's also been spitting a few flakes of snow as well. Dustin is stumbling along with his hands in the pockets of his jacket, making it hard for him to keep up as I quicken the pace. I have to warm my own freezing hands, so I stop and put them under my armpits inside my jacket while I wait for Dustin to catch up again.

"Shit! That's all we need," Dustin says, as a gust of wind and a real flurry of snow hits us in the face.

A snowstorm, or worse yet, a blizzard, is definitely not what Dustin and I need about now. It may not be what we need, but it's what we've got, and this barren, parched land will take as much moisture as it can get. Not that these tiny, dry snow pellets are going to add much more than a trace of precipitation. No, I don't think we're going to get much snow; it's the cold that worries me. The temperature has been plummeting all night. Neither one of us has the right clothes to be out in sub-zero weather. Wish we at least had hats and gloves. It's probably down to freezing already. If the temperature keeps dropping, we might be in real trouble. Like we're not in real trouble, already.

The snow is falling harder as I notice it's getting light. Unlike a clear morning when the light first appears in the eastern sky, this is one of those mornings where the clouds and snow are enough to totally diffuse the growing morning light. The darkness is slowly fading away everywhere, all at once, leaving no way to know which way is east.

"Maybe we should build a fire," Dustin suggests.

I know he is as cold as I am, and there is plenty of brush and pieces of wood scattered along the bottom of the gully, flotsam from long-ago floods, piled high enough in some places that it is hard to climb over. I have to admit the thought of a nice warm fire is tempting, but we can't take a chance on somebody spotting the smoke.

"It would be nice, wouldn't it?" I tell Dustin. "Once we're in Canada, that's the very first thing we'll do. Can you keep going? With this snow and cloud cover, there's probably no need to hide at all today."

"Okay. But I need to rest for just a minute." I can hear the disappointment in his voice. He is disappointed that we can't have a fire and disappointed that we have to keep going, but there is also resolve in his voice. I think Dustin really would follow me anywhere.

Dustin sits down on a large boulder, but I choose to sit on

a sandy spot of ground with my back against the bank of the arroyo. If it weren't so damn cold, I could have a nap. Sitting in the bottom of this frozen ravine, I'm reminded of how cold the winter was when I was sixteen or seventeen years old.

It must have been the winter of '22-'23. I know it was after the world finally got over Coronavirus. After we had all been vaccinated against the plague that so upended our lives in 2020 and 2021. Once Coronavirus could be controlled by an annual vaccine, most everyone, especially my dad, expected a tremendous economic boom. Instead, we got the Great Depression 2.0. Looking back now, it seems strange that Dad didn't blame the Trump government for the depression of the early twenties. But, come to think of it, he didn't blame Trump's government for my mother's death from Covid 19 either. Even though I was only fourteen years old when she died, I knew the government's response to the virus or lack of response, I should say, led to the needless death of thousands, or even hundreds of thousands, of Americans.

Guess I wouldn't have blamed Trump either if I only watched Fox News like Dad and Marv did. I was lucky enough to have a tablet that enabled me to get a better idea of what was really going on in the world. Funny, I didn't realize until just now, those were the years when I truly became an independent thinker. With Mom dead and no one forcing me to go to church, I was able to break the bonds of my early Catholic upbringing; and with my tablet and the internet enabling me to see the world without a Fox News filter, I was well on my way to thinking for myself.

Dad had lost both our home and his home building business by the time that frigid winter hit. Instead of the post-Covid economic prosperity promised by Trump, the U.S., along with the rest of the world, just kept sinking farther and deeper into depression after Coronavirus. The world's social fabric had been too badly torn during the Trump years for the promised economic recovery to ever materialize. Having been a homebuilder his entire life, Dad was one of those who just couldn't adjust to a changing world. A world where fewer and fewer people could afford to buy a home, let alone a new home. Did he blame the government for the total economic collapse? No, like Fox News and ex-president Trump himself, he blamed the "godless liberal socialists" that were "destroying our great country." For people like my dad, it was a simple case of told you so. For them, the depression was a direct result of Trump losing the election to "socialists."

With rental assistance from those terrible socialists who were running the government for those first few years after Trump, we were able to move into subsidized low-income housing. And with food assistance from the local food bank keeping us from starving, we were able to survive that coldest of winters. Many, who were ineligible for governmental aid, mostly those with darker skin than us, weren't so lucky. There was a great dying of homeless people that winter. People who either froze or starved when the temperature plummeted to well below zero and stayed there for weeks at a time. There was no way to know for sure since no one was counting, but more people probably died of starvation and exposure that winter than died of Covid back in '20 and '21. Of course, for my dad and brother, the people who died didn't count anyway. They weren't the "real" Americans. I think that's when I first realized I was never going to fit in as a "real" American, either. And that was before I was entirely sure of my own sexuality.

"Wake up. You're going to freeze!" Dustin is either shaking me, or I am shivering harder than ever. The first thing I notice when I open my eyes is that I'm covered with snow. I must have just passed out from exhaustion.

Dustin is stomping around, shaking the snow off of himself. He must have fallen asleep too. Standing up is agonizing; the stiffness in my joints has been frozen in place. I shake and brush the snow off with numb, frozen hands. The snow has stopped falling, but I'm stomping around in a couple of inches worth in the bottom of the arroyo. Without saying a word, I start walking up the arroyo. We have to get out of here. No matter that it's the middle of the day. Dustin doesn't say anything either as he falls in beside me. Good thing he woke up. He was probably right; if he hadn't been here, I could have sat right there and froze to death, just like those homeless people I was thinking about just before I fell asleep.

"Thanks, Dustin." I stop walking and turn to look at him. "You may have just saved me from freezing to death."

"Guess we're even then," he says, "since you saved me from the gallows." It's so like Dustin to use the term *gallows* when he was scheduled for a lethal injection. Being *saved from the lethal injection* just doesn't quite have the same ring to it, though, as being *saved from the gallows* does. If there's one thing Dustin's good at, it's using the right turn of phrase.

After no more than a quarter of a mile, we come around a bend and, lo and behold, there is an old two-track road coming down into the arroyo through a cut gouged into the side of the dirt bank on our left. The old road comes into the arroyo and then runs up the bottom in the same direction that we've been walking. My first instinct is to use the road to get up out of the wash, but the clouds are thinning out enough that I can see the faintest trace of my shadow on the ground. My shadow is stretched out to my right side. If it's as close to midday as I think it is, we are currently following this arroyo in nearly a due west direction, which means the old road came in from the south.

While I'm working all that out in my head, Dustin is starting up the road to get out of the wash. "Wait," I stop him before he gets too far up the steep bank. "That's the wrong way. Let's follow this road up the arroyo and see if it comes out on the other side."

Calling the old road a road at all is definitely a misnomer. Following the old road up the arroyo is easy on foot but would be nearly impossible in any but the most all-terrain of all-terrain vehicles. There are washouts where the road used to go that could swallow a normal vehicle. Fortunately, the road doesn't stay in the arroyo long before climbing out through another cut in the bank. The bank on our right this time.

The world starts opening up before us as soon as our heads are above the rim of the arroyo. The scene is a brilliant white wonderland. At the top, we stop and take in the scenery. The sun is now breaking through the clouds, reflecting off the snow in a dazzling display of winter sparkle. To the south, the rough country we have been traversing stretches out seemingly to infinity. To the north, where the old road seems to be headed, some pine-covered mountains are no more than five or ten miles away. Maybe that's Canada, is the thought that warms my spirit as the sunshine starts to warm my frozen bones.

It's getting late in the afternoon. Following the ancient road north, we haven't seen any indication of anything all day but wilderness and wide-open spaces. Making our way around one of the rolling hills, we suddenly come upon a gravel road. The road is just a few hundred yards from the first trees at the edge of the mountains. Unlike the old two-track that we've been following through the hills, the gravel road, which seems to run east to west, has been reasonably well maintained. The road doesn't seem like it gets much use, but it appears to have been graded fairly recently, maybe within the past month or so. It must get some use, or why would it be maintained? The old two-track that Dustin and I have been following doesn't intersect with the gravel road at all. At some point in the distant past, the gravel road was built right across the two-track we've been following. The embankment for the newer road was built up right over the old one like the old road wasn't even there.

There is still no sign or sound of anyone except Dustin and me, but climbing up onto the gravel road, I feel the hairs on the back of my neck tingle. This must be the feeling a dog gets when it raises its hackles.

"I don't like this," I tell Dustin as I hurry across the road and back down onto the two-track on the other side.

"Yeah, it seems weird. Pretty nice road to be out here in the middle of nowhere. Wonder where it goes?"

"No telling, but since it seems to only go east or west, I don't want to find out. "North to Canada, I say." I'm starting to feel much better about our situation. The sun is shining brightly, and Canada can't be more than a few miles away.

The snow that fell earlier is all gone. It melted and dried up in no time once the sun came out. The sun is actually hot. We've gone from freezing to sweating in just a few hours. Maybe it's just our pace that is making me sweat. With neither of us saying anything about it, we are practically running toward the trees. I keep looking up at the clear blue sky that was completely overcast just a couple of hours ago. The memory of the drones we heard and the fear of those unheard and unseen drives me to run. The sooner we can get under the cover of some trees, the better.

"Shouldn't we be there by now, Canada I mean?" Dustin asks. We're sitting on a fallen log just inside the edge of the forest, resting after the rush to get here.

"Seems like we have to be close," I say. Neither of us really knows how close we are to the border. Neither of us has ever been to Canada, or this far north at all.

I lean my assault rifle against the log and take off my jacket. It's cooler here in the shade of the trees, but still plenty warm. We must have had a thirty or forty degree temperature swing in the last four hours. The weather has gotten so erratic over the past few years that most people have given up trying to guess what it will be from one day to the next.

I remember when I was young, many of us thought we would be able to do something about climate change, but there were too many others who refused to even try. I think Gen Z, my generation, must have been the first generation willing to make the sacrifices needed to combat climate change. Unfortunately, we were born too late. By the time we were old enough to do anything about it, the damage was irreversible. Some of those who came before tried to get others to act, but far too many people were unwilling to change from a fossil fuel driven economy. They couldn't imagine a world economy that wasn't based on fossil fuels, so they did nothing. The ongoing climate crisis was caused as much by a failure of imagination as it was by the world's reliance on fossil fuels.

My dad was one of those who did nothing. I remember how that was one of the main things he liked about President Trump, the denial that climate change was an issue we needed to do something about. I think for my dad, like many people, it wasn't so much that they didn't believe climate change was happening; they just thought the cure was more harmful than the disease. If the only way to actually do something about climate change was to stop using the fossil fuels that had powered America's rise to greatness, then climate change would just have to happen, and we'd just have to learn to live with the consequences. Well, here we are in 2050, still living, or in many cases, dying with the results. The economic engine that used to drive the world has been obliterated by one crisis after another, and it just keeps getting worse. When I was a kid, people were distraught over the deaths of a couple million people from Covid. The number of people who have died since then, either directly or indirectly, from climate catastrophes is probably in the billions.

My dad, and people like him, had the same approach to Coronavirus early on as they did to climate change. They protested the lockdowns and complained about the way the response was devastating to the economy. At first, the human toll was hardly even noticeable in small-town Colorado. That was before most people personally knew of anyone who had even been infected, let alone died. That was before Dad and Mom both got sick. Before my own mother died.

The strangest thing, though, was how my mother's death didn't even change my Dad's mind. The death of his wife was just one more bad thing that had to be accepted. "Dying is just another part of living," I remember him saying. "If one of those who dies is someone you love, that's just the way it is." Remembering now, even at fourteen years old, I couldn't understand how my own father could think that way. I could never understand why so many people were willing to let millions of others, or even themselves, get sick and die just because they were unwilling to modify their "normal" lives.

I wanted a normal life, too. I wanted nothing more than to go back to school to be with my friends. That was before Mom died; before I did get to go back to school. Before I had to live forever with the guilt of knowing it may have been me that brought Coronavirus home from school. That it may have been me that killed my own mother.

I think that's why we let climate change get to the point that I'm sitting here in shirt sleeves in November in a northern Montana forest, while whole islands have been inundated, and coastal cities are underwater more often than they're dry. People, for the most part, are just unwilling to change until change is forced on them. It's easier to go on trying to adapt to one catastrophe after another than it is to do the hard work of preventing the disasters in the first place.

"Can you believe how warm it is?" Dustin asks. It must be love, or maybe just years spent together; whatever it is, there are more and more times when he and I are on the same mental wavelength. Like we have telepathy, but only with each other, no one else.

"Listen." I can hear something, but it takes a minute for me to realize what it is. We have heard nothing but the sounds of nature for days, but this is definitely not a natural sound. It takes a few seconds to realize it's the sound of a vehicle of some kind, a long way off. As we sit in silence and listen, the sound is getting louder, the vehicle, whatever it is, is getting closer.

From where we're sitting, parts of the gravel road are visible through openings in the trees, which means we could possibly be spotted from that road. "We need to move," I tell Dustin and lead the way uphill into the forest away from the two-track that we've been following.

A hundred yards or so off the road, there's an old fallen spruce tree. When it fell, it pulled up a gigantic root ball, leaving behind a hole in the ground like a natural foxhole. It's perfect. Dustin and I crawl down into the depression. The tree fell toward the dirt road, so the massive pile of earth trapped in the roots hides us from view while leaving just enough small openings at the edge for us to see parts of the old road.

We're no more than settled into the depression when I realize the vehicle is much closer than I thought. There is no engine noise, just the road noise from tires on gravel, an electric vehicle, no doubt. The look of alarm on Dustin's face matches what I feel as we both listen to the sound of the tires coming to a stop out there on the gravel road. Then we hear a sound that sends shivers up and down my spine, the barking and howling of a dog. It sounds like some kind of hound dog that has picked up a scent. I have no doubt about what the scent is that it picked up, and no doubt that some kind of hound is now tracking Dustin and me. How did they know where to search? Where to stop and let out the dog? The drones are the only possible way. I was right to avoid being spotted by surveillance drones, but I guess I wasn't careful enough.

"Let's go!" There is hysteria in Dustin's voice, even though it's just a whisper.

"Too late," I whisper back as I grab the extra magazines for the old Mossberg MMR out of my pack and take up a good shooting position behind the dead tree's root ball.

How many are there? I wonder. It sounds like just one dog, but surely there is more than only one person. Who is it, some kind of border patrol? Whoever it is, they must not have been too far away if a drone just spotted us this morning.

"I'll have to kill the dog for us to have a chance to make a run for it," I whisper to Dustin. "Get ready to shoot back. Somebody is bound to shoot at us when I shoot the dog."

"I can't," Dustin is nearly hysterical and utterly terrified. His face is as white as a sheet, and he's trembling all over.

"Sure you can. Just like I showed you. If you can hit a can, you can definitely hit a person."

I taught Dustin to shoot the .357 while we were holed up at the ranch. Surprisingly, he picked it up incredibly fast for someone who had never fired a gun before. He's not a top-notch marksman like me, but he can hit a tin can at fifty feet with a .357 magnum. Whoever it is with the dog will provide a much larger target than a tin can. Dustin may not have liked being forced to learn to shoot, but right now, I sure am glad he went along with the training.

"I can't," he says again. "I just can't kill another person."

"Okay, at least shoot to scare them then." I don't have time to argue with Dustin. Teaching him how to shoot was one thing; getting him to actually shoot at someone may not be possible.

I adjust my position so I can scan as much of the old road as possible while still being well hidden. Then I train the scope on the opening where the dog should first come into view. Damn it! I hate that I'm going to have to shoot a dog. Not that I won't or can't, but it isn't the dog's fault that it's being used this way.

As I wait for them to come into view, for some reason, my mind wanders back to Dad, teaching Marv and me to shoot guns. I wonder why it came so naturally to me, but not to Marv. I didn't really want to learn how to shoot at first, but Dad insisted. He told us we had to learn to shoot so we could go hunting together. But the real reason, I'm sure, is he wanted me and Marv to be able to defend ourselves. I'm sure my dad thought I'd be defending myself against some Muslim invaders or something, not other Americans. I guess after being a Marine in the Middle East, my dad couldn't help but be biased against Muslims. We never did go hunting together, though. I did go hunting several times with Grandpa, but Dad is the one who first taught me to shoot. Oddly enough, I found that I really liked firearms and shooting. So much so that I joined shooting clubs and won my share of marksmanship competitions. Dad taught us to shoot, and Grandpa taught us to hunt. I was a lot more successful at both than Marv. He became the typical big game hunter who missed as many times as not, while I became the marksman that never misses.

The dog comes into view first. For some reason, I expected

a bloodhound, but it's a black and tan hound dog of some kind. I can easily take out the dog before I even see the handler, but I wait. The hound is pulling so hard on its leash that the handler is practically dragged out into the open.

The man being dragged along by the hound is dressed in desert camo, not a police uniform. He is obviously part of one of the militia groups that seem to be taking over the entire country. The look on his face is one of total surprise when the leash goes slack in his hand as the dog hits the ground. That look of surprise is fitting as my second shot hits him in the middle of his forehead. There has at most been a second between the two shots, but it seems like an eternity. Time slows to a near standstill as I put the cross-hairs on the next man's face, centered on the middle of my brother Marv's forehead. Time stops, my trigger finger frozen.

There's another man beside Marv that doesn't freeze. He fires a shot into the dirt in front of me as he dives behind a tree. Marv is frozen in place, but I still don't pull the trigger. Instead, I train my sights on the edge of the tree the other man is hiding behind. At the edge of my vision, Marv finally moves, turning and running back down the road out of sight.

The deafening sound of a .357 magnum blasting away right beside me breaks the timeless trance. Bark and splinters fly from the tree the other man is hiding behind, and through an opening in the brush, I get just a glimpse of his legs running back down the road following Marv.

"Go – now!" I hiss at Dustin. I throw the extra magazines

that I didn't need back into my pack, sling the backpack over one shoulder and the MMR over the other, and scramble out of the hole right behind Dustin.

"Where? Go where?" He's standing on top of the bank, the .357 still held dangling in his right hand. His face is ashen, and he's looking around with a nearly blank stare.

"Dustin – look at me. Put the gun back in your holster. You still have three shots left; you can reload later." Like Dustin had any idea how many shots he had left. He didn't even know the gun was still in his hand, but telling him he could reload seems to break through the trance. He puts the gun in the holster and looks up at me. The blank stare is gone, replaced by horror.

"You killed him," Dustin says. "You killed that man. And, and the dog," he stammers. "Jesus, I tried to kill someone, too."

"You did what you had to do, Dustin. We did what we had to do. They would have killed us. You know that, don't you?"

We don't have time for this. I'm not sure if there are more than just Marv and the other guy that got away or not, but even if it is only the two of them, they'll probably try to sneak up on us through the woods. The guy with Marv seemed more than competent, probably ex-military. He may have missed once, but I definitely don't want to give him another chance.

Without really thinking about it, I decide to parallel the old forest road just long enough to get away from anyone who might try to sneak up on us. Then, we'll get back down to the road where we can make better time getting away. There is too much deadfall and underbrush to make good time through the forest, and we have to get to Canada as quickly as possible. Getting across the border is the only chance we have left to go on living. We wouldn't even get a trial if they caught us now. They'd just string us up to the nearest tree; if we survived being shot, that is.

We have just made it back down to the old road when I hear it. Dustin practically runs into me as I stop and listen. Then he hears it too. It's the sound of tires on gravel. We're probably a half-mile farther from the gravel road now, but the sound is clear as can be. It's the sound of a car or truck leaving, going back the way it came no more than fifteen minutes ago. The question now is whether or not anyone is still tracking us.

There is probably nothing else in human experience that is quite as relative as the passage of time. My life changed more in the past fifteen minutes than it did in the whole month before. I went from wondering if Marv would lead them to us to realizing the truth in my worst fear; that my own brother really would like to see me dead. I may have told Dustin that Marv wanted me dead, but deep inside, I clung to the hope that it wasn't true. Now, the illusion has been shattered. There is no hope left. Marv is helping them hunt for us, with the sure knowledge that Dustin and I will both be killed. It's a terrible thing to know without a doubt that the only surviving member of your own family wants to see you dead.

I take a seat on one of the many dead trees that have fallen across the old road. Dusk is descending down through the forest. It will be dark soon. I sure hope this old road keeps heading north. It'll be bad enough hiking up the road in the dark, but we have to keep moving, and it would be just about impossible to go cross-country through the forest at night.

"You better reload while there's still light," I tell Dustin. He just looks at me like I'm a stranger and buries his face in his hands.

"You killed him," he mumbles through his hands. "You're a murderer. Twice. You're a mass murderer."

There is nothing I can say. I don't consider myself a murderer at all, let alone a mass murderer. I have never killed anyone except in self-defense. Doesn't Dustin understand that they will kill us? That deputy that I shot back in Colorado may not have killed Dustin himself, but he was damn sure willing to help carry out the death sentence that the judge handed down. In my eyes, it was self-defense both times. I had no choice; I had to kill. Hell, I feel worse about shooting that poor dog than I do about shooting its handler. The dog didn't know any better, but the man should have.

"Give me the ammo," I tell Dustin as I reach over and take the revolver out of his holster.

~

Damn, I'm tired. We've been on our feet for at least twenty-four hours now. Morning's light is starting to filter down through the trees. Dustin is stumbling along beside me, doing his best to keep up. He has hardly said a word since the shootout last night. All night long, we have walked in silence, following the old dirt road, lost in our own thoughts. The road is impassable except on foot. I'm sure we aren't being followed, but why not? Why did Marv and the other guy just take off? Maybe the other guy was wounded. Maybe Dustin actually did shoot someone, hard to believe, but maybe.

Nearly exhausted, I climb over another dead tree that fell across the old road. Like life itself, there have been many roadblocks for us to climb over or go around on this old two-track road. Trees that have fallen across the road, slides, and washouts where the road cut into the sides of hills and mountains as it worked its way ever north. In some places, the forest has nearly reclaimed the old road, and we have to work our way through thickets of young aspen trees. It's been a somewhat twisting and winding route through the mountains, but through all of the twists and turns, the road has always led to Canada. I know we must be getting close now. Will our journey be over when we get across the border, or will that be just the beginning?

As I keep putting one foot in front of the other, I think about how my whole life has led me to this place and time. Like this old road itself, there have been twists and turns and roadblocks along the way. But through it all, my life has always led to right here, right now. That's what I've been thinking about all night long, my life, and all I've been a witness to in forty-four years of living. So much has changed, and most of it not for the better. I'm not even fifty years old yet, and in my lifetime, I have been a firsthand witness to the decline and fall of the country where I was born.

When I was a boy, we were taught that we lived in a democracy where the people would always decide what was best for our country. An illusion that was shattered for me at an early age, when I came to understand that America was actually ruled by a minority. Long before the Aryan Christian Nationalists came to total power, the United States was ruled by a right-wing minority. They mostly called themselves Republicans back then. They were the so-called silent majority or moral majority that never did comprise an actual majority of citizens in the United States. They may have been a minority, but they did wield most of the power. They ruled by stoking religious and cultural differences and then ratcheting it up a notch, by stoking fear of the other. We were told our country was founded on the principle of religious freedom for all. That may have been the founding principle of our country, but what it meant in practice was the imposition of a select interpretation of Christian values and white superiority on everyone else. There were always those who wanted to practice variations of Christianity. And there were those who followed Islam or other religions. Everyone who wished for something different than fundamentalist evangelical Christianity made the same mistake. They all failed to realize that freedom of religion can't last forever unless every religion is willing to allow freedom from religion itself. With religious doctrine and dogma being used for centuries to control populations and to grow and maintain power, the concept of freedom from any religion has always been anathema to all organized religions. Every organized religion I know of has always wanted more than just the freedom to practice their own religion. They always wanted as many others as possible to also practice their particular religion. Most religious leaders and many of their followers have wanted the U.S. to be governed according to the tenets of their own specific faith, but none could ever pull it off. Not until the ACN was formed, that is.

As I've been walking along thinking about religion and the Aryan Christian Nationalists, the road has been making one of its long slow curves around a wooded hill. The thick forest suddenly gives way as the curve in the road leads around from east to north. Dustin and I find ourselves looking out of the forest into a totally cleared swath of land about a hundred yards wide. The cleared band runs due east and west, and it has a well maintained barbed wire fence right in the center. We've made it. This has to be the border, though I expected a much more substantial fence. I expected a chain-link fence with razor wire on top, like the pictures of the border I've seen on the internet. Guess this area is just too remote to have that kind of security. There is no gate or opening where the fence crosses the remains of the old road. The road is a relic of an earlier time when there probably wasn't even a border fence. A time when the border between the U.S. and Canada was hardly a border at all. When people could go back and forth at will in these remote parts. Back then, in the early twentieth century, most people in these parts probably didn't even know where the border was or which side they were on.

The relationship between Canada and the United States certainly has changed over the past century. It's 2050, and most of that change has all happened in just the past twenty or thirty years. I wonder if the world has ever changed as much in a single lifetime as it has in mine. I wonder how much longer mankind can survive without even more drastic change. How much longer can our species survive without reversing much of the damage that we humans have inflicted on ourselves and our world?

Dustin and I are both stopped at the edge of the clearing. I'm wondering what kind of sensors or cameras might be monitoring the fence line when all hell breaks loose. In my peripheral vision, I see Dustin falling backward at the same time as I hear the sound of a gunshot. My body reacts faster than I would have ever thought possible. I'm lying on the ground behind a tree looking through the scope of my MMR before even having time to think about it. Only then do I realize that it wasn't just one gunshot. It was a flurry of shots that came from the area I'm now scanning through the scope. I can't see anyone or anything out of place, just a few clumps of brush scattered about in the tall grass waving in the light morning breeze.

After an eternity of lying prone and staring through the rifle's scope, I see something. At first, it's just a slight movement. Then one of the short growths of brush in the clearing stands up. The camouflage the man is wearing is so good I never would have seen him if he'd just kept lying still. As it is, it's an easy shot that takes him right through the camouflage face paint as he starts walking toward us. The man's gun goes off as he hits the ground. No doubt, the reflex action of a dead trigger finger.

The chaotic noise of gunshots gives way to nothing but surreal silence until I hear a soft moaning sound coming from Dustin behind me. I want to go to Dustin, but I just keep looking through the scope of the rifle, searching for any other vigilantes that might be out there. I'm sure the camouflaged man wasn't alone.

The man in the camo face paint wasn't Marv. I don't even know if it was the same guy that ran away with Marv earlier, but it must be the same guy. Marv has to be out there somewhere. Who else would know to ambush us right here at the border? Who knows? Maybe Marv and his companions were part of a larger group. Maybe they called in our location to someone else. What if there's a whole fucking army out there, not just one or two more assholes? If that were the case, I'd be dead by now. Maybe the camo dude was it. It seems like I've been looking through the scope forever, staring at nothing but the grass, the brush, and the fence, that fence marking the border, so tantalizingly close and still so far away.

Dustin moans again behind me. Still no sign of anyone else out there. I carefully study every clump of brush through the scope, but none of them is anything but just that, just clumps of brush. I know it hasn't even been a minute, but it seems like I've been staring through the scope for hours. I hear movement behind me and spin quickly, gun at the ready, but it's only Dustin. He's sitting up, staring wide-eyed at the gun I'm pointing at him. I lower the gun and crawl back toward him, careful not to stand up and make myself a better target than I already am.

"Stay down," I hiss at Dustin as I crawl toward him, terrified that someone will shoot him again. Dustin's face is as white as snow, like the blood from his face has all drained out through the hole in his shoulder, soaking the front of his shirt. I know the hole in the back of his shoulder will probably be much worse. Exit wounds always are.

Dustin either doesn't hear me, or he's in such a state of shock that he doesn't realize he could be shot again. He's still sitting up when I get to him. I rip open his shirt to see how bad it is. The small hole in the hollow of his left shoulder, just below the collar bone, doesn't seem big enough to produce the amount of blood that has soaked his shirt, but it's the only wound. It's a relief to see that the bullet hole is barely oozing now. Fearing the worst, as gently as I can, I pull Dustin's shirt down around his arm to see how much of the back of his shoulder has been blown away. It hasn't. Thank god. The exit wound isn't much bigger than the entry. It must have been a jacketed bullet, maybe one of those designed to pierce Kevlar. Whatever it was, it looks like it went straight through and doesn't appear to have hit any arteries. The hole in the back of Dustin's shoulder is about the same size as the one in front. It, too, is hardly bleeding now. I thank the stars that it's probably not a life-threatening wound. The relief I feel is tempered by the feeling I have that there's still someone else out there. A lone vigilante wouldn't have ambushed us like this.

Just as Dustin's eyes open wide to stare in terror at something over my shoulder, I hear whatever it is he's seeing. I throw myself sideways, rolling over and coming up with my rifle pointed directly at Marv. He is just a few yards away with a rifle aimed right at me. In a single instant that might as well be an eternity, I start to squeeze the trigger even as I'm sure that he is pulling his. I can't do it. I can't kill my own brother. I remember a time, back when we were young, when Marv was my hero. A time when we were best friends as well as brothers. A time when he would have given his life to protect me. I can no more take his life now than I could have back then. I lower my rifle, expecting to be dead in an instant. Instead, Marv just sneers at me, while carefully keeping the gun aimed right at my head.

"You always were weak, you gutless queer," he says. The hatred in Marv's eyes is overwhelming. How can one harbor that much hate toward one's own brother? "I should have killed you as soon as I found out you were gay," he says. "You're nothing but an abomination. Your kind doesn't deserve to live."

I can actually see the movement of his finger as it starts to squeeze the trigger. I hear the blast, knowing that I shouldn't. I see Marv fly backward, his rifle harmlessly firing into the air above me. It wasn't the sound of Marv's gun I heard. It was a

.357 magnum revolver going off close enough to damn near deafen me. I turn my head to see Dustin. He is sitting in the same position as when I examined his wound. Only now, he's holding the big revolver in his right hand, still pointed to where Marv is lying dead on the ground.

~

"You need to get out of here. It isn't safe anymore."

It's not what I expected John to say immediately after getting back from town. Dustin and I have been living and working here on John Dixon's farm for a couple of months now. Since just a few days after the shootout at the border. Once we were in Canada, we made our way north and east until we saw John putting up hay all by himself. It seemed like a lot of work for one man, so I asked him if he could use some help. It must have been obvious to John that we needed help more than he did, but he agreed to let us work for room and board. At first, Dustin's shoulder wouldn't allow him to do any hard physical work, so he took care of the domestic chores while I helped John in the fields.

It was an arrangement that seemed to work well for all of us. John had lost his wife to cancer years ago, and his only son was part of Canada's border security force. Canadian Border Security was responsible for making sure Americans stayed on their own side of the border. Not an easy task with the longest land border in the world. The Canadians weren't worried so much about keeping refugees like Dustin and me out. Canadian Border Security was far too busy repelling American militia groups. The militia groups were raiding into Canada with ever-growing impunity.

"They raided Eastend last night," John said by way of explanation. "Said they were looking for a couple of American escapees. They didn't find any, but that didn't stop them from terrorizing the townsfolk before leaving. I don't know what would have happened if they'd found anybody harboring American fugitives."

I could see that the raid on Eastend had frightened John, as well it should. If the vigilantes found out that he had aided and abetted fugitives from American justice, they'd be just as likely to string him up as they would us. The look on John's weathered face told me how hard it was for him to have to throw us out.

"I don't know about Eastend," I tell him, "but I know if they find Dustin and me here, they'll hang all three of us. We'll get out of here right now. Putting you in danger is the last thing either of us would want."

John knew, of course, that we were fugitives. Probably the very ones the militia was looking for. John had been extremely kind, and we had not deceived him one little bit about what and who we were. When we first met John, we told him that we wanted to go into town to apply for asylum. He convinced us that it was probably not a very good idea. He said the Canadian government had been forced into agreeing to send back American criminals. John and even the Canadian courts might sympathize with us for killing the men we did. However, in the court's eyes, we would still be legitimate suspects in ongoing murder investigations in the United States. The courts would have no choice but to send us back.

"You need to get farther away from the border, somewhere up north," John says. "I'm sorry, I really am."

I have come to know John quite well over the past couple of months, and I can see that he isn't really afraid for himself. He is mostly scared for Dustin and me. John knows as well as I do that we won't have to worry about Canadian or American courts either one if the vigilantes find us.

"I'm sorry too, John. I'm sorry we put you in danger. Guess we thought once we made it to Canada, we'd be free to start over."

"God damn Americans," there is real anger in John's voice, anger mixed with sorrow. "You know, I'm old enough to remember when our two countries were the closest of allies. How the hell did it come to this?"

I feel John's pain and anger, but I don't have an answer. I don't have an answer to anything. I don't even have a country. Dustin and I are American refugees with absolutely nowhere left to run. The worst part of all is the knowledge that even if Canada granted us asylum, it wouldn't last forever. The Aryan Christian Nationalists won't allow a liberal, secular country to exist on their northern border. Not for long anyway. They won't stop until they've overrun the entire world. And with Muslim extremists hell-bent on taking over the world themselves, not to mention the Russians and the Chinese, this is bound to end very badly for everyone.

Most, if not all, of the religions I know anything about have some kind of prophecy of an Armageddon at the end of the world. Most, if not all, have knowingly or unknowingly been working for centuries, not to stop that apocalypse, but to facilitate it.

As I head back to John's house to get Dustin, I wonder where we can go now, other than simply farther north. Where can anyone go to escape Armageddon? In a cataclysm that is worldwide, national borders mean nothing. The real question for humanity is not who will escape at the end of the world. The real question is, who, if anyone, will survive?

If you enjoyed American Refugees, please take just a moment to give it a rating or review. Reader's reviews and comments mean the world to me. I read them all and cherish each and every one.

Thank you so much for reading!

Social media is not my style, but I love hearing from readers:
marcus.dean@lastditchpress.com
or
www.marcuslynndean.com

OTHER BOOKS BY MARCUS LYNN DEAN

THE THERMALS OF TIME SERIES

THE THIRD AND FINAL BOOK OF THE THERMALS
OF TIME WILL
BE AVAILABLE IN THE SPRING OF 2021

Made in the USA
Coppell, TX
08 November 2020

40991271R00042